MY NEW SHIRT

Cary Fagan

Illustrated by
Dušan Petričić

Tundra Books

Published in Canada by Tundra Books,
75 Sherbourne Street, Toronto, Ontario M5A 2P9

Published in the United States by Tundra Books of Northern New York,
P.O. Box 1030, Plattsburgh, New York 12901

Library of Congress Control Number: 2006909132

LIBRARY AND ARCHIVES CANADA CATALOGUING IN PUBLICATION

Fagan, Cary
    My new shirt / Cary Fagan ; illustrated by Dušan Petričić.

ISBN 978-0-88776-715-9

1. Gifts—Juvenile fiction. I. Petričić, Dušan II. Title.

PS8561.A375M9 2007   jC813'.54   C2006-905772-9

We acknowledge the financial support of the Government of Canada through the Book Publishing Industry
Development Program (BPIDP) and that of the Government of Ontario through the Ontario Media Development
Corporation's Ontario Book Initiative. We further acknowledge the support of the Canada Council for the Arts and the
Ontario Arts Council for our publishing program.

ONTARIO ARTS COUNCIL
CONSEIL DES ARTS DE L'ONTARIO

The illustrations for this book were rendered in watercolor on Arches paper
Printed and bound in China

1 2 3 4 5 6   12 11 10 09 08 07

In memory of my grandmothers,
Adele Fagan and Sylvia Menkes.

C.F.

For Aleksa and Lazar,
two unbelievable boys.

D.P.

Mom

Me

"Oh, Da-a-a-v-i-i-d!"

calls my mom in a sing-song voice. "It's time to visit your bubbie. Today is your special day and she has something for you."

In my room, I play with my dog, Pupik. Usually I like to visit my bubbie. Her apartment always smells of cinnamon and it's just above the Kuni Lemmel Bagel Shop, which makes the best bagels in the world. I like her neighbors, Mrs. Morgenstern and Mr. Zangwill and the Katz sisters. I like visiting my bubbie. Except for one day a year. My birthday.

Bubbie

Mr. Morgenstern

Mr. Zangwill

Katz sisters

Pupik

"Can I bring Pupik?" I ask.

"Of course," Mom says. "Bubbie likes Pupik, too."

We get into the car and drive to the city. Pupik wants to stick his head out the window, but he's too short and has to climb on top of me.

At last we get to Bubbie's street. Along the sidewalk is a fish store, a candy shop, a fruit stand, a café, a hair salon, and the Kuni Lemmel Bagel Shop. Dad parks the car.

"Yoo-hoo! Dovila!" calls my bubbie. I look up, past the iron fire escape to the window. And there is Bubbie, holding up a box and smiling.

"I have something for you, David. A surprise!"

Something, yes. A surprise, no.

We enter by the door beside the bagel shop and go upstairs. My bubbie waits at the top. She is holding *the box*.

"Not so fast," Bubbie says, as if I were trying to snatch it from her hands. "Come inside first."

Bubbie's apartment is small but spotless. My mom says that Bubbie makes cleaning an art, and Dad says that germs are afraid even to try and come in.

"David," Bubbie says, "before I give this to you, I want to say what a good and wonderful and terrific boy you are. May you continue to give such joy to us all." She gives me a kiss and hands me the box.

"Go on, don't be shy," Bubbie says. "Open it."

What else can I do? I open it.

Inside the box is tissue paper. And inside the tissue paper is a shirt. Not a baseball shirt. Not a T-shirt with a picture of Anti-Gravity Man or a stegosaurus on it. Instead, it is a bright white shirt with buttons. A *stiff* shirt with an even *stiffer* collar. It is the sort of shirt that your parents want you to wear buttoned up because it makes you look like a "little gentleman." The sort of shirt that makes you squirm and pull and shift and twitch.

A shirt just like the one Bubbie gave me last year. And the year before that. And the year before that.

"How gorgeous!" my mom says. "A new shirt! David, it's just what you need."

"Everybody looks good in a white shirt," my dad says. "You're going to look like a little gentleman in that."

"I got it a size larger than last year," says Bubbie. "Go on, David. Try it on."

I stare at my parents. Do they really like the shirt? How does a kid who thinks like me become a grownup who thinks like *that*?

This white shirt is identical to all the other white shirts that Bubbie has given me. It even has the same scratchy label that will rub against the back of my neck.

For a moment, I close my eyes. In my mind, I see a closet. An *endless* closet, winding upwards from my room and going right through the roof into the sky. Hanging in this closet is a row of white shirts, a shirt for every year of my life as I get older and older. . . .

"*DAVID!*" screams my mom. "What has happened?"

I open my eyes and see Mom and Dad and Bubbie staring at me, openmouthed. Pupik is barking. The shirt is not in my hands.

"Where is the shirt?" I ask.

Dad says, "You threw it out the window!"

"I did?"

"I'm sure it was an accident," my mom says.

"Quick!" cries Bubbie. "To the window!"

We rush to the window and look out. There's the shirt, hanging on the rail of the fire escape!

"I'll climb out and get it," I say.

"So that you can fall and break your neck?" scolds my mom. "I don't think so, Mister. Your father can get it."

"But I'm wearing my good shoes," Dad says. Mom gives him a look. He sighs and takes a step toward the window. But before he has a chance, Pupik runs past us all and leaps onto the fire escape. He pulls the shirt off the rail and holds it gently between his teeth.

"Good dog, Pupik," says Bubbie. "Now, bring it to me."

Pupik growls.

"Bad dog!" Dad says sternly. "Bring it here right now."

I've never seen my bubbie move so fast. She runs out of the apartment and down to the sidewalk. Mom and Dad and I are right behind her.

"There!" Mom points. And we all see Pupik hurrying away as fast as his short legs will go, the shirt waving in his teeth. I, too, say, "Bad dog," although not so loud that Pupik will hear me.

Halfway down the block, Mrs. Morgenstern is watering her vegetable garden. Pupik goes skidding through the dirt and water, dragging the shirt behind him.

"He's dragging the shirt right through the mud!" yowls Bubbie. "Oy, it's a disaster!" But she doesn't give up. She runs after Pupik, and we run after her.

Pupik bounds toward the Sisters Katz Hair Salon. It must be a quiet day because Doris Katz has brought her chair outside and Nettie Katz is sitting in it. Doris is dying Nettie's hair.

"I'm going to look forty years old again," says Nettie.

Pupik doesn't know where to run, so he jumps up into Nettie's lap. Nettie screams as the shirt flips onto her head. Pupik leaps off Nettie, lands on his stomach, bounces up, and takes off again with the shirt.

"What a catastrophe!" wails my mom.

At the outdoor café, Pupik gets tangled up in the chair legs. "Surround the café!" commands Bubbie. "We'll corner him."

At one table, just like every afternoon, sits Mr. Zangwill.
Everybody knows that Mr. Zangwill believes eating a bowl of bright
red borscht soup is the secret of good health.

Mr. Zangwill suddenly feels something under his feet.

He jumps up, the table tilts over, the borscht slides down.

"Oh, no!" moans my mother, covering her eyes with her hands. "Borscht stains!"

My mother should not have covered her eyes. Pupik runs right past her.

This time it looks like Pupik is really going to get away. But at that moment, Sydney Lemmel, whose parents own the bagel shop, wheels out a giant bin of fresh bagels. When he sees Pupik barreling toward him, he freezes. Pupik can't slow down, so he jumps.

He lands in the bin. Bagels fly everywhere.

I rush to the bin and take my dog in my arms.

Bubbie picks up the shirt.

"Just look at it," says Mom. "It's a *shmatte*, a rag."

"Such a shame," says Dad, biting into a poppyseed bagel.

"Oh, well, Bubbie," I say, trying to sound sad. "It's the thought that counts."

"You're just trying to make me feel better. Don't you worry. If anyone can get this shirt clean, it's me."

Bubbie leans over and pinches me on the cheek.

"What a precious boychick you are."

Back at her apartment, Bubbie goes to work. Bubbie has so many cleaners, her laundry room looks like a science laboratory. She takes the shirt and sprays it. Powders it. Scrubs it. Soaks it.

Then into the washing machine it goes. She pours in the detergent. She pours in the bleach. The washing machine begins to whir. While we wait, Bubbie serves tea and apple cake.

Pupik sulks in the corner until Bubbie scratches him behind the ears and says, "I forgive you, Pupik." She even gives him a piece of apple cake, too. We pass the time talking about relatives from long ago. "Your great uncle Mort," says Bubbie. "There was a man who knew how to wear a shirt."

The rest of us stay where we are as Bubbie puts the shirt into the dryer. Then we hear the clank of the ironing board and the hiss of the hot iron. Finally, Bubbie comes back. She takes the shirt from behind her back.

"Ta-*da*!"

The shirt is just like new, as white and as stiff as before.

"A miracle!" my mom says.

"I've got to admit it, you're the maestro of washing," my dad compliments her.

"Try it on, David. We'll see how good you look," Bubbie says with a grin.

Pupik whimpers. I take the shirt and hold it in my hand. I can't help it when once more my eyes close. In my mind I see that closet, winding high into the sky, white shirt after white shirt after white shirt....

"DAVID!"

The shirt has gone out the window. I swear I don't know how. There it is, caught on the fire escape, just like before.

"I'll climb out and get it," I say.

"So that you fall and break your neck? I don't think so, Mister. Your father can get it."

My father looks down at his shoes, but doesn't say anything. Just as he's about to climb out the window, Pupik leaps past him. Pupik grabs the shirt and scurries down the iron stairs.

"Should we go after him?" I ask.

"Of course," Bubbie says, heading for the door. But then she stops, turns, and smiles at me.

"How about," she says, "Next year I get you something different for your birthday?"

"Okay, Bubbie." I smile back.

And we're off.